MARMADUKE RIDES AGAIN!

By Brad Anderson and Dorothy Leeming

SCHOLASTIC BOOK SERVICES
New York Toronto London Auckland Sydney Tokyo

ISBN: 0-590-08072-5

23 22 21 20 19 18 17 16 15 14   0 1 2 3/8
Printed in U.S.A.   06

"HANG ON, MARMADUKE! HANG ON!"

"Hey, Pop, Marmaduke's as long as he is high!
Then how come he isn't square?"

"Keep an eye on him! He's the one that
almost ran us over last night!"

"Honest, Mrs. Winslow, I said they had to go
to bed . . . but HE said they didn't!"

"It's not his begging I mind so much as that
'or else' look in his eye!"

"Marmaduke, you've made a mistake!
This ISN'T Billy!"

" 'Dear Mr. & Mrs. Snyder. . . . By the time you
read this, we will be headed for Florida.' "

"For the LAST time, will you let me see if
that meter reads 'Expired'?"

"You just chewed up my last chance for a
'B' in history!"

"We're having a circus and we need a tiger!"

"What happens if he's unclaimed for 30 days?"

"Pass it down, but skip him if you can!"

"It's all my fault, really! I asked him
to give me his paw!"

"I think I know what happened to your
wristwatch, Pop!"

"I think it's the first time he's ever seen
a dog THAT big!"

"The note says: 'We're stuck. . . . Fill the can
with gas—and the dog with candy!' "

"Good boy! Now keep him there till I go
get some money!"

"Now I know why it's called a 'pup tent'!"

"Oh, he brings in the paper all right . . . a page at a time!"

"Down lower, Marmaduke! It's not easy get-
ting on without a saddle!"

"He won that ribbon at the dog show . . .
for leaving!"

"I don't mind his playing with my slippers
. . . but not while I'm in them!"

"I gave him twin engines, but I still can't
get him off the ground!"

"But, Mommy, all Marmaduke did was yawn!"

"Look at it this way . . . if it wasn't for
Marmaduke, Snyder would never
get any exercise!"

"I dare you to come in HERE and say that!"

"Would you come with me to the insurance office?
They might believe TWO of us!"

"Thanks, Pop! Now I'll be able to look Marmaduke
in the eye when I talk to him!"

"We were watching the man making cotton candy...
and you know how nosy Marmaduke is!"

"Which is Marmaduke's?"

"But that's not the stick I told you to fetch!"

"That's what I'd do if I could get away with it!"

"We've had him since he was only THIS high!"

"I don't think you're TRYING to remember
where you live!"

"Watch it! I don't like the way he's
eyeing your hat!"

"One good thing . . . there's lots of him to bandage!"

"Mr. Winslow, I want to thank you for helping put my boy through college!"

"You chewed it in two, so now you can just
hold it until I get these clothes off!"

"Where would we be if he had sense enough to come in out of the rain?"

"Mister, you want my friend here to teach 'em
how to bark? He's GOOD at it!"

"Do ya mind?"

"As long as we have an expert handy, let's ask
HIM about the quality of this steak!"

"Marmaduke wants to be bounced next!"

"Marmaduke found us a better lunch than the
one I packed!"

"Stop looking, Phil! I just found
the other slipper!"

"Nonsense, Snyder! Marmaduke KNOWS he's not
allowed in your fish pond!"

"Guess what, Phil! The kids taught Marmaduke
a new trick today!"

"See? I TOLD you it was a dog!"

"Other dogs bring their leashes for a walk.
. . . HE brings the car keys for a ride!"

"Was he baying at the moon again last night?
Our yard is full of Snyder's shoes!"

"Marmaduke's nice like that. . . . He's boosting
Pedro's self-confidence!"

**"Just taking him to Colby's Car Wash
for a b-a-t-h!"**

"Now, let's see, Mr. Winslow. . . . You have a wife,
a son, a daughter, and whatever THAT is!"

"Pop, remember that trick you said was so
hard to do?"

"Mr. Snyder tried to shoot a grape off his head!"

"When my boss invited us to a formal dinner,
it didn't include YOU!"

"You bad, bad dog! NOW I'll have to put in
a little overtime at $7.50 an hour!"

"My advice to you is, 'Cut down on dog biscuits and stop chasing cars!' "

"He's a good turner, but a terrible jumper!"

"Play along with him, Phil. . . . I think he just
wants to show you something!"

"Gangway! We're movin' our clubhouse
to Ronnie's backyard!"

"Well, it's better than taking him for a walk
around the block every evening!"

"Stop blowing on my coffee. . . . I'm not
THAT late!"

"We could never get him to wear a muzzle, so
we tell him it's a catcher's mask!"

"Five bars of soap comin' up, Pop!"

"You SHOULD hide after what you did to
Mr. Snyder's moss roses!"

"Careful with that pepper, Billy! Remember what
happened the LAST TIME Marmaduke sneezed!?!"

"It was MY fault, ma'am! Honest! All MY fault!"

"Marmaduke plays right, center, and left field . . .
all at once!"

"I found an easier way to give Marmaduke a bath!"

"Relax! It's just Marmaduke going up the stairs!"

"Gee, Mom, maybe you don't recognize me,
but you ought to know him!"

"This ought to keep him from barking for a
while. . . . I'm feeding him peanut butter!"

"That's Marmaduke! Don't bother with him!
We list him as a pony!"

"Well, he sure solved my 7 apples
minus 2 apples problem!"

"I guess he still remembers the sun roof we
had on the old car!"

"Sure he knows how to play. You oughta hear
him bark out signals!"

"We went to a rummage sale and, boy,
did he rummage!"

"No, we DIDN'T build a guest house!
That's a doghouse!"

"Where did you GET that?"

"How many gallons per minute?"

"If it's excitement and drama you want, why not bathe Marmaduke?"

"Now, now, dear, how could HE know
it's a spite fence?"

"Hon, I know what happened to that lemon pie...
and it was too tart, anyway!"

"Just make sure he knows it's TOUCH football!"

"Odd-looking caddy Winslow has with him today."

"There! Now we have plenty of room in the car!"

"The charge is romping through a supermarket!"

"But he's CRAZY about babies!"

"He NEVER has trouble finding the car, does he?"

"Mr. Snyder tried to run away with our ball, Pop!"

"I'll flip you to see who goes down first!"

"See, Billy? This is why I don't like him
to go fishing with us!"

"Why shouldn't he feel secure? He
outweighs me by 40 pounds!"

"Uh . . . we brought our own lifeguard!
That's O.K., isn't it?"

"I know how you feel, fella! Traffic affects
me the same way!"

"Whenever HE comes to the door for the mail, don't argue. . . . Just GIVE it to him!"

"We-e-l-l, he MIGHT be mine! What's he done?"

"All right, let's try it again and no nonsense
this time.... Let me see your tongue!"

"Actually, it's worse since we got
a color TV set!"

"We'll get rid of him . . . soon as he sees this soap!"

"He doesn't seem to get the hang of this
master-pet relationship!"

"This is the place I was telling you about, Marmaduke!"

106

"He isn't much protection, but what
a conversation piece!"

"Barbie, drop the pill in first . . .
then the meat, Billy!"

"For Pete's sake, watch where you drop it!"

"It's your own fault for chewing up our tent pole!"

"Are they kidding? With YOU sitting on my foot?"

"Stop worrying, Harriet! These puppies are a completely different breed!"

"But, Officer, your radar must have picked up that big dog that passed me on the road!"

"Keep the motor running!"

"Start reciting flavors.... He'll bark when you
get to the one he wants!"

"I gotta say this for him . . . he adds a lot
of variety to a fireman's life!"

"Well, do we go in or don't we?"

"Better take him along to help close it for
the trip home!"

"Give my pal here anything he barks for!"

"If he starts PLAYING that guitar,
we're MOVING!"

"You shouldn't have told him to speak!"

"That's just his midafternoon snack!"

"Will you GO HOME! That's the FIFTH bus
that's whizzed by here!"

"Let's just say they gave!"

"Tiptoe, Phil . . . and DON'T let those
car keys jangle!"